HELLO! WELCOME TO THE FABUMOUSE WORLD OF THE THEA SISTERS!

Thea Sisters

Hi, I'm Thea Stilton, Geronimo Stilton's sister! I am a special reporter for <u>The Rodent's Gazette</u>, the most famouse newspaper on Mouse Island. I love traveling and meeting new mice all over the world, like the Thea Sisters. These five friends have helped me out with my adventures. Let me introduce you to these fabumouse young mice!

Colette has a real passion for fashion. She loves to design her own clothes in her favorite color, pink.

Violet loves studying and learning new things. She is a fan of classical music and dreams of becoming a famouse violinist someday.

Pamela loves pizza so much she eats it for breakfast. She is a skilled mechanic who can fix just about any motor she gets her paws on.

PAULINA is shy and loves to read about faraway places. But she loves traveling to those places even more.

Nicky is from the Australian Outback, where she developed a love of nature and the environment. This outdoors-loving mouse is always on the move.

Thea Sisters

Thea Stilton

MOUSEFORD ACADEMY
A FASHIONABLE MYSTERY

Scholastic Inc.

Copyright © 2010 by Edizioni Piemme S.p.A., Palazzo Mondadori, Via Mondadori 1, 20090 Segrate, Italy

International Rights © Atlantyca S.p.A.

English translation © 2015 by Atlantyca S.p.A.

The publisher does not have any control over and does not assume any responsibility for author or third-party websites or their content.

www.geronimostilton.com

Published by Scholastic Inc., 557 Broadway, New York, NY 10012. SCHOLASTIC and associated logos are trademarks and/or registered trademarks of Scholastic Inc.

Stilton is the name of a famous English cheese. It is a registered trademark of the Stilton Cheese Makers' Association. For more information, go to www.stiltoncheese.com.

This book is a work of fiction. Names, characters, places, and incidents are either the product of the author's imagination or are used fictitiously, and any resemblance to actual persons, living or dead, business establishments, events, or locales is entirely coincidental.

ISBN 978-0-545-87096-2

Text by Thea Stilton
Original title *Chi si nasconde a Topford?*
Cover by Giuseppe Facciotto
Illustrations by Valeria Brambilla and Francesco Castelli
Graphics by Chiara Cebraro

Special thanks to Anna Bloom
Translated by Anna Pizzelli
Interior design by Becky James

10 9 8 7 6 5   19

Printed in the U.S.A.   40
First printing 2015

BEACH DAY!

The halls of Mouseford Academy were completely deserted. Classes had ended for the weekend, and the building was as **QUIET AS A MOUSE**. The sun shone brightly, and an **ocean breeze** drifted through the windows. The lack of students was easy to explain — this was the first real beach day of the year!

Most mice flocked to the **wide** beaches on the east coast of Whale Island, but

SEASHELL BEACH

WHALE ISLAND

Mouseford students and professors liked Seashell Beach best. It was a small cove with calm water surrounded by rocks that were good for **climbing**.

Every year, Nicky volunteered to be a weekend lifeguard. She loved waking up before everyone else and jogging to the deserted cove. In the early morning, Nicky

had the beach all to herself.

That morning, however, Nicky had company. As soon as she got to the cove, Nicky noticed a **STRANGE RODENT** sitting on the rocks, staring out to sea.

As soon as the stranger heard Nicky approach, she **JUMPED** to her feet. The mouse quickly put on her wide-brimmed

Who is she?

straw hat, adjusted her **SUNGLASSES**, and took off running like she was on an exercise wheel.

Nicky shrugged. How strange!

ON THE ROAD!

At Mouseford Academy, the other Thea Sisters were also *RUNNING* — they were really late!

"Hurry, mouselets! We'll miss the bus!" Paulina called, her voice ECHOING in the empty hallway.

"Colette took too long putting on her sunscreen!" Pam grumbled, lugging a heavy bag FULL OF TOWELS.

"You're supposed to apply sunscreen before you go outside!" Colette exclaimed.

"Well, what about the twenty minutes you spent picking out a *bathing suit*?" Pam asked.

"There are no shortcuts where fashion is

concerned!" Colette panted, clutching her **PURPLE** beach bag.

The Thea Sisters jogged out of the building and saw a big group boarding the beach bus.

"Finally, you're here." Elly sighed as soon as she saw the THEA SiSTERS climb on the bus.

Shen and Craig were on the bus as well. They were already wearing their **bathing suits**.

"Mouselings, we'll have to SPLIT UP to get seats," Pam said. She waved at Paulina, who had already been **PUSHED** to the back of the bus by the crowd.

Who's your favorite singer? Mine's Catty Perry!

An old lady sat in front of Paulina, next to a tourist wearing a brightly colored Hawaiian shirt.

"Oof." The lady sighed. "Every summer gets worse! There are more and more tourists, and no seats on the bus!"

Are you from around here?

8

The rodent in the Hawaiian shirt turned to her. "Are you from around here?" he asked. "I bet you know **EVERYONE** on the island."

Paulina noticed that he was wearing a professional-looking camera.

"My friend Anna absolutely **loves** this island," the tourist continued. "She has blue **EYES** and short blonde hair. She arrived a few days ago . . . maybe you've seen her?"

The old **MOUSE** shook her head and dug a magazine out of her bag.

The mouse with the camera didn't give up. He spent the whole trip asking everyone around him if they'd seen his friend Anna.

Finally, the bus reached the first stop. **"TURTLE BEACH!"** the bus driver called.

In a few **short** minutes, more than half the passengers had gotten off. The

Thea Sisters could **finally** sit next to one another! The mice chattered *excitedly* as they dropped into their seats. Soon they would be at the beach enjoying some **FUN** in the **sun**!

SEASHELL BEACH

At the cove, Nicky stood on a rock with a good view of the beach. She peered at the sky through a pair of **BINOCULARS**.

On Whale Island, the weather could change quickly. Nicky wanted to be sure there were no **THUNDERSTORMS** coming.

Nicky turned to look at the hills behind her and caught a glimpse of a remote cottage named Cheddarton House.

Cheddarton House was well known on the island, but **no one** had lived there for a long time.

"Strange," Nicky said to herself. "It looks like the cottage WINDOWS are open.

Maybe the owner finally rented it out."

As Nicky **WATCHED**, someone stepped onto the balcony. She immediately recognized the mysterious mouse who had been sitting on the **beach** that morning.

Just then the bus drove up, *honking* loudly.

BEEP! BEEP! BEEP!

Nicky immediately spotted her friends among the crowd of rodents headed to the beach and **hurried** to meet them.

"Our favorite lifeguard!" Colette shouted in greeting. She dropped her huge bag on the ground and **hugged** Nicky enthusiastically. "Look how many of us came today! You'll have your paws full keeping an eye on everyone!"

Nicky laughed. "If you wanted the beach to yourself, you shouldn't have taken so long getting ready!"

Nicky thought about the **straNge** mouse she'd just spotted through her binoculars. "This morning when I got to the beach, there was someone here early. But she *RAN AWAY* when she saw me! I think she's renting Cheddarton House."

The others turned to look at the cottage, but they couldn't see much.

Craig bounded up and interrupted them. "We're playing **BeaCH VoLLeYBaLL** after lunch! You should join us," he squeaked. "It's going to be the game of the century: professors versus students!"

Craig's **ENTHUSIASM** was so contagious that none of them could resist!

After lunch, the students set up a net. Craig

volunteered to be the captain of the student team, and Professor Robert Plotfur led the professors. The two captains **shook paws** to start the game.

On Craig's team, Pam and Paulina got into position. Professors Ian Van Kraken and Anna Aria took their spots on the other side of the net.

As the lifeguard, Nicky had to stay on the rocks to **WATCH** the swimming area, but every once in a while, she turned to see how the game was going.

It was an exciting matchup. The students got an early lead. Pam and Paulina were excellent players. But the professors were good, too. They came back **STRONG** — and won the whole thing!

"Rematch!" Craig demanded, eager to redeem himself.

Violet checked the time and gasped. "It's four o'clock! We have a newspaper editorial meeting at the academy!" she exclaimed.

"Mouselets, we're late! We have to go!"

THE SUMMER ISSUE

The two teams agreed to postpone the REMATCH until the following day. "The news waits for no mouse!" said Professor Plotfur.

The Thea Sisters made it back to school in RECORD time. When they finally burst into the classroom where the rest of the newspaper staff was meeting, everyone else was already there.

"Sorry we're late!" **Violet** cried, sitting down at the table.

Tanja, the editor in chief, smiled. "Don't worry; you deserved some **beach time**! Ruby's not here yet, either." She rolled her eyes.

Ruby Flashyfur always preferred to arrive fashionably late. She waltzed in a few minutes later in a cloud of perfume, plopped into a chair, and sighed. "I hated to leave my new **superdeluxe hot tub** to come to this meeting."

Tanja tapped the table with her pen. "Let's focus, mouselings! We only have two weeks before the *special* summer issue comes out, and we need some fabumouse ideas."

I'm here!

"We could *INTERVIEW* the village fishermice," Paulina suggested.

Ruby snorted. "That would be great — if we wanted to put all our readers right to sleep!"

"If you don't like that idea, Ruby, why don't you suggest something?" Pam said.

Ruby tossed her hair. "Well, now that you mention it, I do have the perfect idea." She paused dramatically. "We should do an article on the most exclusive hot spot for the rich and fabumouse — my mom's yacht!"

"We featured your mom's yacht last year," Tanja reminded her. "Don't you remember? You wouldn't stop talking about it."

Ruby turned as **RED AS A GOUDA CHEESE RIND**, and the other mice broke into giggles.

"Who else has thoughts?" Tanja continued.

"The summer issue is our big chance to do something creative!" Tanja's eyes lit up like she was staring down at a gourmet cheese plate.

The room got very quiet. The newsmice stared at their paws, thinking carefully.

"Why don't we go to dinner?" Elly

We need something special!

suggested finally, breaking the silence. "We can pick up tomorrow morning after some well-aged cheddar and a good night's sleep. That always helps me."

Tanja shrugged. "Sounds good. I want to hear some fabumouse ideas from all of you tomorrow!"

FLASH OF GENIUS!

After taking their **BEACH GEAR** to their rooms, the Thea Sisters met at the cafeteria and got in line for food. Pam, who was hungry after a busy day at the beach, filled up her **TRAY** with lots of **TRIPLE-CHEESE PIZZA**.

Colette **shook** her head. "Haven't you ever heard of a **WELL-BALANCED** meal?"

"Sure!" Pam replied with a big smile. "Look at my tray — it's perfectly balanced on my paw!"

Paulina laughed and carefully surveyed her **veggie** options. She was famouse for her elaborate, super-creative salads. She

stopped suddenly and turned to Colette. "I've got the perfect idea for the summer issue — **healthy** food to eat at the beach!" she exclaimed, beaming.

"An article like that would certainly be **useful** to Pam!" Colette teased. Then she stared at Pam, suddenly serious. "Oh, dear — I think you got sunburned today!"

Oh, Pam!

Pam touched her face and grimaced. "My snout feels like cheese toast!"

"But maybe that could be an article in the summer issue, too," Colette continued. "**DIY** treatments for sunburn!"

"You are a genius, Colette!" Paulina said, **clapping** her paws together. "The

This table looks free!

summer issue can be all about having fun in the sun while staying healthy! Skin care, fur treatments, good food — the possibilities are endless!"

The friends found an empty table and sat down to eat. Pamela took a bite from an ENORMOUSE SLICE of pizza.

"YUM!"

Violet tasted her **cheddar** broccoli soup and set her spoon down. "I just can't stop thinking about the summer issue," she said. "I like the healthy summer fun idea, but I have another thought. What was the most **important** event that happened this school year?"

"Professor Camille Ratyshnikov's arrival, of course!" Paulina replied with no *hesitation*.

"The professor's new theater class certainly got everyone talking," Colette agreed.

Violet nodded. "Right! In my *opinion*, since the school year is ending, we should do a story on Professor Ratyshnikov and the new performing arts program!"

Violet started to explain her **idea** in more detail. Colette pulled out a pen to jot down their brainstorming notes.

None of them noticed that someone close by was eavesdropping! Connie and Zoe had sneakily found a table right behind the Thea Sisters, **HIDDEN** from view by a giant

plant. When they heard Violet mention the newspaper, their ears perked up.

Violet continued explaining her **PLAN**. "We could start by interviewing the professors in the new **PeRfoRMiNG aRtS** department. Then we could describe how a show is set up and what goes on behind the curtains. We could even explain how important the stage design, costumes, and LiGHTiNG are."

"That's enough material to fill ten summer issues!" Pam cried. "If you want, I could be your *photographer*."

Paulina kissed Violet on the cheek. "This will be the best summer issue yet!"

Zoe listened to these last words and GRINNED at Connie. "Their summer issue suggestion is the best idea since SLICED CHEESE . . . but they won't be the ones who take credit for it!" Zoe whispered.

The two mice grabbed their trays and hurried off to find Ruby. On their way out of the cafeteria, they bumped into their friend Alicia and quickly filled her in.

"Why, that's genius!" Alicia exclaimed. "We have to let Ruby know."

Nicky Gets Suspicious

After listening to Connie and Zoe's report, Ruby was quiet for a few moments. "A special issue on Ratyshnikov's new program," she said. "The Thea Sisters came up with a really wonderful idea!"

Connie, Zoe, and Alicia exchanged confused glances. Was Ruby really complimenting the Thea Sisters? IMPOSSIBLE! Ruby quickly put them at ease. "Too bad they don't have enough style to do this idea justice." She put her snout in the air and sniffed.

Hmmm...

"But the Thea Sisters came up with the idea, so they'll be the ones who get to be in charge of the special issue, right?" Alicia asked.

Ruby glared at the mouseling. "Don't worry about that! I already know how I'm going to FIX that little problem . . ."

While Ruby was busy plotting a takeover of the SUMMER ISSUE, the Thea Sisters were still in the cafeteria, waiting for Nicky to return from lifeguarding.

"There's our rescue mouse!" cried Colette, looking up from her notes.

"I'm exhausted!" Nicky said, slumping into a chair. "I had a great time, but the beach got really crowded." She took a bite of the grilled cheese sandwich she'd picked up. It was her favorite — Brie and green apple.

"Did we miss anything after we left?" Paulina asked.

"You'll never guess who came to the **beach**!" Nicky said with a t*w*in*k*le in her eyes.

"Who?" they all chorused together.

"The headmaster!" Nicky finally revealed. She giggled at her friends' **amazed** expressions.

"I can't believe it! He **NEVER** goes to the beach!" Pamela said.

"Professor Ratyshnikov talked him into going," Nicky continued. "She even got him to play **PADDLEBALL** with her on the beach. You wouldn't **believe** how good Professor Ratyshnikov is!"

"I wish I could have seen them play!" Colette said.

"You're in luck!" Nicky pulled her phone

out of her **Pocket** and showed her friends the screen. "I took a picture!"

The mouselets peered at Nicky's phone, amused.

"This picture should be on the **FRONT PAGE** of the summer issue!" Paulina teased.

"I wish!" Pamela laughed. "Imagine the headline!"

HEADMASTER HAS A BALL AT THE BEACH!

Violet scrolled through the other images on Nicky's phone. "Who is this?" she asked, stopping on a picture of someone in a FLOWERED skirt.

Nicky squinted at the image. "That's some rodent from out of town. She was asking everyone lots of questions. She wanted to know if anyone had seen a **newcomer** to the island with short blonde hair."

"What a coincidence!" Paulina said. "This morning on the bus, I overheard someone else **asking** about the same person!"

"Who do you think they're looking for?" Pam wondered.

"I actually think I might know," Nicky said. "It must be the same mysterious blonde **MOUSE** I saw sitting on the rocks this morning. The one who's renting **Cheddarton House**!"

RUBY'S FABUMOUSE IDEA

The next morning, the Thea Sisters went to the newspaper meeting with a long list of notes. They had stayed up late brainstorming and couldn't wait to present their ideas to the others.

Tanja welcomed them with a triumphant smile. "Great news, team! Ruby came up with a marvemouse idea last night!" she exclaimed. "She suggested we make the summer issue all about Professor Ratyshnikov's new performing arts department! What do you think?"

The Thea Sisters couldn't squeak a word.

Violet finally found her voice. "It's a

fabumouse idea. We would love to help Ruby work on it." Violet suspected Ruby had stolen their idea, but she didn't want to accuse her without proof.

"We'll find a **little** something for you to do," Ruby said, smirking.

"There's plenty of work, mouselets." Tanja clapped her paws together.

The Thea Sisters exchanged disappointed glances as they took their seats, tails **drooping**. Somehow, Ruby had figured out their big idea for the summer issue — and now she was going to be in charge of handing out all the assignments!

Later that **afternoon**, the friends went back to **Seashell Beach** to cheer themselves up. There, they filled Nicky in on what she had missed.

"This stinks worse than **old string**

cheese!" Nicky said. "But we won't let Ruby ruin the summer issue for us. I'm sure we can find a way to **work** with her."

"Ruby or no Ruby, I need a swim!" Pam declared.

The Thea Sisters headed to the **water**, and Nicky went back to her duties. Peering through her **BINOCULARS**, she glimpsed something moving outside Cheddarton House. The odd tourists from

the previous day were lurking outside the gates!

"I would love to know what those two cheese curds are up to," she **mumbled**.

A **coMmotion** on the beach brought Nicky's attention back to her friends. She could tell that the team selections for the **volleyball** rematch were in full swing.

Yesterday's game had been so much fun

TEAM PROFESSOR!

that now everyone wanted to play! It was difficult to narrow it down, but Craig and Professor Plotfur managed to choose two teams of six players each. The game got started, and the professors took an early lead.

"Come on, mouselets!" Pam cheered. "Don't let the professors MELT your cheddar!"

TEAM STUDENT!

PROFESSOR SPARKLE SPIKES!

SHEN'S QUICK SAVE!

PROFESSOR ANNA ARIA'S TERRIFIC SERVE!

CRAIG'S KICK!

The PLAYERS from both teams gave it their best, until disaster struck. **SLAM!**

Craig failed to stop a **spike**. He tried desperately to keep the ball from hitting the sand in front of him, and he ended up kicking it accidentally.

The ball bounced along the ground and disappeared behind some rocks. A moment later, a shriek rang out.

"OUCH!"

A MYSTERIOUS MOUSE

Professor Sparkle ran to see who had been hit as Nicky watched.

"That's the **MYSTERIOUS** mouse from *yesterday*!" Nicky exclaimed.

The blow from the ball had knocked off the *blonde* mouse's hat, and she was rubbing her sore head. Nicky could finally see her **Face** for the first time. *I think I've seen her before*, Nicky thought.

At first, the blonde mouse looked angry. But when she saw Professor Sparkle walking toward her to **apologize**, she quickly jammed her **HAT** back on her head and

darted away from the beach.

Professor Sparkle came back with the volleyball, shrugging.

In a rush to ESCAPE, the blonde mouse started up a dangerous route back to her cottage. Worried, Nicky called to her friends. "Catch up to that mouse! She doesn't know about the **WASHED-OUT** path!"

The mouselets immediately ran after the stranger, waving their arms and shouting at her to stop. But the mouse kept going.

The blonde mouse had begun **climbing** the rocky path that led from the beach to Cheddarton House. At first glance, the route looked **safe**, but it dropped off steeply after the first turn.

"*COME BACK!*" Colette cried.

"IT'S DANGEROUS UP THERE!" Violet added.

But the stranger kept walking. "Leave me alone!" she yelled back, her snout in the air.

Colette and Violet **waved** more frantically — the blonde mouse had reached the most dangerous spot. She was too **DISTRACTED** to notice the trouble she was in.

"I'm sorry, but I'm not giving any interviews — **HEEEELP!**"

The **MYSTERIOUS** mouse slipped

off the path! She managed to grab a bush, but her feet dangled high above the shore. Nothing stood between her and a steep drop to **SHARP** rocks and ROUGH water.

Heeeelp!

THE THEA SISTERS TO THE RESCUE!

Violet and Colette **RUSHED** to help the stranded stranger. Each mouse grabbed an arm, but they weren't **aBLe** to drag her up.

the stranger shouted again. "I'm scared of heights!"

"Try not to panic, and don't look down!" Violet said. "Help is on the way."

Nicky didn't waste any time. She ran to the **toolshed**, grabbed two strong ropes, two harnesses, and a couple of carabiners. Then she took off running up a shortcut to reach her friends.

When Nicky found them, she was panting. "Hold on! I need to set up my rope."

Expert mountaineer that she was, Nicky knew how to make strong **kn©ts**. She secured her rope and started climbing down to the blonde mouse.

"I'm going to put a harness on you," she explained. "That will make pulling you up as easy as spreading **cream cheese**!"

The blonde mouse couldn't even squeak. She stared in horror at the water below her and started **trembling** like a cheese wrapper. If Violet and Colette let go of her now, she would certainly fall!

Just then Paulina and Pamela arrived on the cliff, too. They had seen Nicky dash off with ropes, so they stopped the volleyball game to follow their **friend**.

Don't worry!

Nicky tossed up the rope that she'd tied to the tourist's harness. Paulina caught it, and the four friends standing on the upper edge of the cliff started *PULLING* ■➤ with all their strength.

"Come on, mouselets!" Pam urged them. "We can do it!"

In no time at all, the mysterious mouse had her 🐾🐾🐾🐾 back on solid ground!

"Thank you," she whispered, regaining her **breath**. "You saved my life! Those rocks would have made Swiss cheese out of me if you hadn't rescued me."

Violet stared at her. "You're Anna Winmouse!" she blurted out. "The famouse editor in chief of **COSMOUSE**, the most prestigious fashion magazine that's ever existed!"

"Of course!" Nicky smacked her forehead. "That's where I've seen you before. Your picture is in the latest issue of *Cosmouse*!"

The editor in chief looked **embarrassed**. "That's me. But if you only just recognized me . . . does this mean you aren't reporters?"

"We hope we will be someday!"

Paulina confessed. "But right now we're just students at Mouseford Academy."

"Is that why you ran away?" asked Colette.

"You thought we were **reporters** looking for a scoop?"

HiDDEN iN PLAiN SiGHT

Anna Winmouse put her sunglasses back on. "My behavior must have seemed really strange to you!" she said. "But the press has been terrible recently. The more I try to **GET AWAY** from reporters, the pushier they get!" The famouse editor shook her head. "When I **SAW** you and heard you shouting, I thought I had been discovered!"

It's been terrible!

"Unfortunately, I think someone really has found you," Nicky said. "Yesterday two **STRANGE** mice were asking a lot of questions, and today I saw them outside Cheddarton House!"

"Oh no!" Anna Winmouse groaned and twisted her tail between her paws.

"Wait," Pam said. "Why don't we continue this conversation in the shade with a nice cold soda?"

Nicky had to go back to her LIFEGUARD duties, but the OTHERS headed toward a secluded inlet on the beach.

"I'll keep watch with the binoculars," Nicky promised.

Sitting in the shade with a cold soda in her paws, Anna Winmouse explained her problem to the girls. "Managing a fashion magazine requires a lot of hard work. You have to assign stories, choose the best **articles**, pick out the most beautiful pictures . . ." She trailed off. "But there's more! The magazine has been so successful that everybody has been asking me for interviews and advice. My life has gotten so busy that I don't have time for what I love most: researching the newest fashion TRENDS and sharing them with the public."

Violet nodded. "Sometimes success can be stressful!" she agreed.

Anna Winmouse finished her soda and continued her story. "A couple of weeks ago, I decided to get away and hide in a quiet, out-of-the-way place. When I found Cheddarton House, I thought it would be perfect! As soon as I arrived on Whale Island, its cozy atmosphere immediately made me feel better. I've already come up with lots of new ideas for the magazine!"

"You found fashion inspiration here?"

Colette asked, her eyes shining.

Anna Winmouse smiled at her. "With this fabumouse landscape, of course!" But then the smile disappeared from her snout. "I need quiet and privacy to be able to focus. If the reporters don't stop harassing me, the magazine is doomed!"

THE PERFECT HIDEOUT

Paulina stood up. "There's only one place on the island where we know you'll be left alone — **MOUSEFORD ACADEMY!**"

"The academy?" Anna Winmouse asked, surprised.

"Paulina is right," Pam agreed. "Our headmaster would never allow reporters inside!"

"We should go talk to him right away!" Colette said. She and Pam leaped to their feet. They stretched their paws out to help up Anna Winmouse.

"Thanks so much, mouselets!" Anna Winmouse looked relieved. She was very happy to follow them back to school.

When the group got back to Mouseford, they didn't have any **trouble** persuading Headmaster Octavius de Mousus to let Anna Winmouse stay.

"How could we refuse the famouse editor of *Cosmouse*? I completely understand your need to work in peace," he said, feeling *sympathetic*. "Nobody will bother you here."

Then he rushed off to arrange a *quiet* room for her.

But the arrival of the Thea Sisters' new guest did not go **unnoticed** . . .

Ruby had immediately spotted the Thea Sisters and a mysterious blonde rodent entering the headmaster's office. Ruby had lingered next to the headmaster's slightly open door and heard Pamela ask for an **autograph**.

She must be someone **FAMOUSE***!* Ruby thought. She quickly snapped a **picture** of the stranger with her phone and texted it to Alan, her **very efficient** assistant. Ruby just had to find out who she was.

Alan's reply came quickly. "That's Anna Winmouse — the famouse editor of *Cosmouse*," Ruby read. "**RUMOR** has it that she's doing **TOP SECRET** research for the magazine."

Welcome to Mouseford!

Just then the office door opened, and Ruby saw the Thea Sisters walk out with Anna. Ruby flattened herself into an alcove so they wouldn't spot her.

This is an amazing opportunity, Ruby thought. *I could interview her for the summer issue — and get her to endorse Flashyfur brand products in* Cosmouse!

I could even **model** *for the photo shoot.* Ruby grinned. *This is my chance to be the big cheese!*

PAM'S PLAN

Now that the headmaster had allowed her to stay at **MOUSEFORD**, Anna Winmouse felt **energized**. The academy was the perfect place to collect new ideas — she felt like a brand-new rodent!

In order to get to work, though, she needed her **COMPUTER**. But she wasn't sure how she could retrieve it from her cottage without being noticed by the two **snoops** lurking outside Cheddarton House. Luckily for her, the Thea Sisters were happy to **HELP**!

They called Nicky, who was still at the beach, for an update on the reporters.

Nicky looked through her **binoculars**.

"I can see them! They're hiding behind a bush, waiting for Anna to come back."

Pam came up with a foolproof plan to outsmart the reporters. "We'll take my **JEEP**. Once we get there, Paulina and I will keep them busy. In the meantime, the rest of you can **sneak** into the cottage and grab everything Anna needs."

The Thea Sisters and Anna Winmouse piled into Pam's jeep. Just before they reached the cottage, Pam stopped to let the others off.

Then she and Paulina drove up to the cottage GATES, stopping in front of the bush where the two snoops were hiding. "Yoo-hoo," Pam called to them. "Can you help us figure out where we are?" She opened up a **MAP**. "We got all turned around!"

While Pam had the reporters distracted with her map, Anna, Violet, and Colette SNUCK into the back of the cottage. They grabbed Anna's computer and crept back out — without the reporters noticing anything!

RUBY'S PLAN

Half an hour later, Anna Winmouse and the Thea Sisters were back at Mouseford, safe and sound.

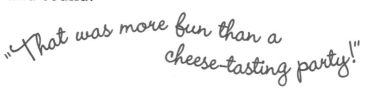

"That was more fun than a cheese-tasting party!"

Anna exclaimed as they walked to her room. She had tears in her eyes from laughing so much.

When the group got to Anna's door, however, a **SURPRISE** was waiting for them. Anna had barely put her hand on the doorknob when it was flung open, revealing Ruby standing inside!

"Welcome back!" Ruby cried, grabbing

Anna by the arm. "You can go now," she said **coldly** to the Thea Sisters. "I can take care of our guest now."

The Thea Sisters were speechless.

"**WOW!**" Pam finally exclaimed, poking her snout inside. "I had no idea the guest rooms at Mouseford were this **fancy**!"

"Usually they're not!" Ruby said, looking pleased. "I **took the liberty** of making a few upgrades."

Right this way!

But . . .

The room had a FOUR-POSTER bed, heavy velvet curtains, and a huge WOODEN table topped with a big basket of fresh fruit. Large bouquets of **bright** flowers filled the air with perfume.

Ruby invited Anna Winmouse to make herself comfortable. Then she hurried to close the door, leaving the Thea Sisters standing openmouthed in the **hallway**.

Anna Winmouse collapsed into a **soft** armchair, tired from her long day.

Seeing Anna look so relaxed, Ruby **decided** this was her chance to make her big pitch. *Anna is sure to be impressed by my ideas!* Ruby thought.

Ruby reached into a huge bag she'd brought with her. It was filled with **lotions**, shampoos, **makeup**, and perfume samples — all Flashyfur brand!

"I just love *Flashyfur*, don't you?" Ruby said. Without waiting for an answer, she opened a shampoo bottle and waved it under Anna's **snout**. "Smell the **strawberries** in this shampoo — you can almost taste them! Surely your *Cosmouse* readers would love to read about it!"

Anna Winmouse frowned. "I really appreciate your welcome, but I'm going to take a **nap** now." She got up from her chair, took Ruby's arm, and led her toward the door.

"There are just a few more things I thought you'd like to see," Ruby continued, undeterred. She reached into her bag and pulled out a folder of **photographs**. "I would be the perfect mouse to **model** Flashyfur, don't you think?"

Anna Winmouse smiled **sweetly**, opened

her door, and gently nudged Ruby over the threshold. "Good-bye. Thanks for the flowers," Anna said as she closed her door, leaving Ruby standing in the **ACADEMY** hallway.

"This is *not* over," Ruby grumbled to herself.

The next day, newspaper duties were keeping everyone very busy. Since Ruby was in charge of the SPECIAL summer issue, she was in her element bossing around the other mouselets. She kept making Paulina redesign the same page layouts **over and over** again, and she had Pam and Violet rewrite all their interview questions for the professors.

Not good enough!

"I'm going to be here awhile," Paulina whispered to Violet and Pam. "You might as well go eat lunch while you can!"

They took her advice and headed off to the dining hall. Just as they were getting in line, Tanja rushed up to them, looking worried.

"Have you done your **interviews** yet?" she asked.

Oh no!

"No, why?" Violet said. "Professor Aria and Professor Plié are leaving for a two-week training program today," Tanja explained. "If you don't do their interviews **right now**, they won't make the issue!"

"Cheddar biscuits!" Violet cried.

"But Ruby had us rewrite all the questions!" Pamela exclaimed.

Tanja shook her head. "I don't know why she didn't tell you."

Violet and Pam **THANKED** Tanja and rushed off to find the professors. It was just like Ruby not to warn them that their interviewees were going out of town!

How much longer is this going to take?

The rest of the THEA SISTERS were also running into trouble. Ruby had enlisted her Ruby Crew to keep them busy with fake assignments so she could have Anna Winmouse **ALL** to herself!

Connie kept an eye on Colette, who Ruby had doing research for the summer issue in the **library**. Zoe stuck close to Nicky, who was looking through Professor Van Kraken's DVDs for a short article on **summer** sea life. At this rate, the Thea Sisters would have their **PAWS** full all day!

Just a few more!

EAT UP!

Once the Thea Sisters were **distracted**, Ruby could dedicate the entire afternoon to befriending Anna Winmouse. As soon as they were friends, Anna would certainly want Ruby to model Flashyfur in *Cosmouse*.

If I can also persuade Anna to do an exclusive interview for the summer issue, that's even better! Ruby thought. *This will be the best issue yet!*

Ruby searched **online** for clues about the famouse editor. Every time Ruby thought she'd learned something useful, she rushed off to try it on Anna.

"Anna Winmouse loves **chocolate**!" declared an article about **COSMOUSE'S**

editor in chief. So Ruby showed up at Anna's door with an enormouse tray of delicious candies.

"Anna Winmouse is a fabumouse golfer!" trumpeted another headline. So Ruby donned her cutest golf gear and invited Anna to join her for a round.

Anna Winmouse barely had a moment to herself all afternoon because Ruby was constantly knocking on her

Try a chocolate?

Want to golf?

door. Anna was almost at her **wit's end** by dinnertime.

Ruby had discovered that Anna Winmouse was a real **foodie**, so she planned to offer her an elaborate evening meal. At six o'clock, Ruby arrived at Anna's room with Jacques Fondue, her mother's French **CHEF**. A long line of **waiters** followed him, pushing carts carrying **five-star** dishes.

Everyone is in a good mood after a **good meal**, Ruby thought.

Anna Winmouse did look **DELIGHTED** as an array of cheddar fondue, Stilton soufflé, and Parmesan crisps was placed in **FRONT** of her. "It all smells so marvemouse, Ruby!" Anna sighed and clasped her paws together.

Ruby's plan didn't go quite as well as she'd hoped, though. Anna Winmouse spent the whole meal talking to the chef. Ruby

couldn't get one *squeak* in!

Ruby was **furious** as she slunk out of the room after dessert, her tail between her legs. "Cheese and crackers!" she hissed. "I still haven't even shown her my photographs!"

But Ruby wasn't ready to give up yet . . .

Ta-da!

That smells delicious!

AMBUSH!

Over the next few days, the Thea Sisters stayed busy with newspaper duties. After a week of hard work, they finally stopped by Anna Winmouse's room to take a break and say hello.

"We thought you might like to see the observatory," Violet said. "We can take a scenic walk through the woods. You can see the entire island from up there!"

"That sounds great!" Anna replied, turning her computer off and grabbing a STRAW HAT. "I could use a break to stretch my tail!"

Ruby was lurking near Anna Winmouse's room when the THEA SISTERS made their suggestion. When the group headed out, Ruby ran to call the Ruby Crew. The Thea Sisters' outing had given her an idea!

The walk to the observatory was a little long, but the ocean views were SPECTACULAR. The group paused at every scenic overlook to take it all in.

"That ocean! Not to be cheesy, but it makes me feel so alive!" Anna exclaimed.

When Anna and the Thea Sisters finally reached the top of FALCON'S PEAK, the sun had begun to set.

"There's the observatory!" Pamela called, pointing to the DOME up above.

They hadn't reached the entrance yet when a series of bright lights exploded around them.

Three reporters had jumped out from the surrounding bushes and were **taking photographs**! They blinded the Thea Sisters and Anna Winmouse with all their Flashbulbs.

A barrage of questions followed.

"Why are you hiding out at Mouseford Academy?"

"Is it true you're quitting *Cosmouse*?"

Anna Winmouse was **speechless**.

Suddenly, a car **ROARED** up the path and skidded to a stop. The passenger door opened wide. **IT WAS RUBY!**

"Get in — quick!" Ruby urged Anna.

Eager to escape, Anna leaped in, and the car **TOOK OFF** down the winding road. The reporters piled into their pink car and took off after them.

SURPRISE PARTY

In a moment, the Thea Sisters were all alone.

"Holey cheese!" Pamela exclaimed, rubbing her eyes. "Those flashbulbs hurt my eyes!"

"How did they know that we would be here?" Colette wondered.

Paulina shook her head, confused. "I don't know."

"This might SOUND CRAZY, but one of those reporters sounded really familiar to me," Violet said.

Violet had a pretty good HUNCH . . .

After finding out about the Thea Sisters' planned observatory trip, Ruby had immediately gathered the Ruby Crew. She had them disguise themselves as reporters and wait for Anna outside the observatory. That way, Ruby could arrive just in the NICK OF TIME to save the day!

In Ruby's car, Anna Winmouse started to worry about the Thea Sisters. "We have to go back for them!" she insisted.

"They're fine," Ruby assured her. "There's no need to get your tail in a twist." She sped toward the beach and stopped the car in front of a large, stylish boat: Rebecca Flashyfur's **YACHT**.

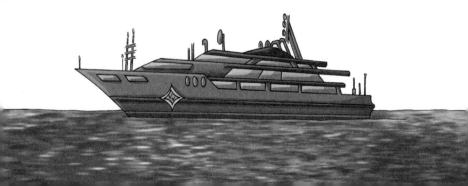

"Let's hide on board my mom's yacht!" Ruby called, **climbing** out of the car. "It's okay. She's a **BIG FAN** of yours!" Ruby said when Anna Winmouse hesitated.

The quiet, darkened yacht seemed **safe** enough, so Anna followed Ruby out of the car. But as soon as Anna set a paw on board, all the lights came on, and a round of applause erupted.

CLAP CLAP CLAP CLAP CLAP CLAP CLAP CLAP CLAP

"Welcome to my yacht!" Rebecca Flashyfur called, sweeping over in a shimmering gown. "You're the **big cheese** this evening at my exclusive Flashyfur party!"

Anna Winmouse was very **embarrassed** by all the fuss. She thanked Ruby's mother for her hospitality but asked Ruby to drive

her back to the **ACADEMY**.

"I'm not feeling well," she said apologetically.

Ruby was **FURIOUS**! *How rude!* she thought on the way back to school. *I talked my mom into throwing that party just for her!*

A FLASHYFUR NEVER GIVES UP!

The next morning, Anna Winmouse met up with the THEA SISTERS in the academy library.

"Why don't we try taking a relaxing trip again?" she asked them. "What do you say about a day at **Seashell Beach**, mouselets?"

Unfortunately for them, Ruby was once again listening to their PLANS for the day.

Ruby crouched behind a nearby BOOKSHELF and

Today is the day!

smiled. Today was the day she was finally going to get an interview out of Anna Winmouse! A FLASHYFUR NEVER GIVES UP! she thought.

"You'll either talk to me," Ruby whispered, "or face a crowd of crazy **reporters**!"

ESCAPE ON THE HIGH SEAS

That afternoon at Seashell Beach, clouds moved quickly across the sky, and the waves crashed onto the sand. Nicky watched them with concern.

"Don't go out too far!" she called to the swimmers. "I think a storm might be coming!"

Most rodents stayed out of the rough water, though, preferring to read or play games on the sand.

Anna Winmouse was enjoying the ocean breeze from under an umbrella. Her peace and quiet didn't last long, though. She sat up suddenly when she heard loud voices.

"THERE SHE IS!" "ARE YOU SURE?"
"IT'S ANNA WINMOUSE!"
"SHE WON'T GET AWAY THIS TIME!"

Anna Winmouse turned to see at least a dozen reporters charging at her!

"How did they find us?" Colette **YELLED**, running to help Anna.

"Someone must have called them!" Pam replied. "We have to get Anna out of here. I'll get the **Jeep**!"

"Ms. Winmouse!" she heard someone yell. "This way!"

Pam turned around and saw Ruby and a muscular rodent invite Anna to get on a **pedalboat**.

"Not you again!" Anna cried. But going with Ruby seemed to be the best option, so she **JUMPED** on board.

"Trust me," Ruby reassured her. "With

Barry Burrata at the pedals, they'll never catch us!" Ruby tapped Barry's shoulder, and he started pedaling furiously.

Back onshore, the Thea Sisters quickly devised a plan to keep the reporters from spotting Anna on the boat.

Paulina grabbed the editor's iconic **STRAW HAT** from where she'd dropped it in the sand and climbed into Pam's jeep.

Colette pointed at her, shouting, "There is Anna Winmouse — she's *GETTING AWAY*!"

The reporters immediately took off after Pam and Paulina as fast as their paws could take them.

In no time at all, the pedalboat carrying Anna Winmouse was far out to sea. Nicky tried to signal to Ruby and Anna to turn back, but they couldn't see her. Nicky blew her lifeguarding whistle and waved at the pedalboat.

"Where are they going? The undertow is strong today — and they're not wearing life vests!" Nicky frowned. **BLACK CLOUDS** had started to gather overhead. A **STORM** was brewing.

ROUGH WATERS

The waves started to **toss** the pedalboat back and forth. Even though Barry was pedaling with all his might, the boat wasn't getting anywhere.

"Faster, you massive mozzarella!" Ruby shouted. Suddenly, a **LOUD NOISE** startled them.

Puff... puff...

CRACK!

The boat's RUDDER had broken — now there was no way to steer!

"What are we going to do?" Ruby cried. "The

waves are going to make Swiss cheese out of us!" For the first time since they'd set out, she looked *worried*.

"Let's not panic!" Anna Winmouse said, clutching the side of the boat for support. "Let's put on **LIFE VESTS**; they should be around here somewhere."

Barry opened the compartment that held the vests, but just then a gigantic **WAVE** crashed right on top of them.

SPLAAAASH!!!
SPLAAAASH!!!

When the pedalboat recovered, they could see the life jackets floating among the waves, UNREACHABLE.

Barry looked scared. "I can't swim!" he sobbed.

Lucky for them, Nicky was on her way! She had Colette call the **COAST GUARD**, while she and Professor Sparkle pushed a lifeboat into the water.

Nicky and Professor Sparkle paddled **fiercely** through the rough sea. They cut through the waves like a warm cheese knife slicing through Gouda. "We'll help stabilize their boat and make sure it doesn't capsize before the coast guard arrives," Nicky explained as they got close to Anna and the others.

EASIER SAID THAN DONE!

The waves tossed the pedalboat up and down, but Nicky was finally able to tie a rope on to its railing. Hooked together, the boats were less likely to tip over.

A SNEAKY SWITCH

In the meantime, the reporters onshore had realized their mistake and returned to Seashell Beach. They watched the arrival of the coast guard boat intensely. Photographs of *Cosmouse*'s editor in chief being **RESCUED** from a boat accident would be front-page news all over the world. When the coast guard boat landed, all the cameras went off at the same time.

The first rodent down the steps of the **COAST GUARD** boat was Ruby, soggier than a slice of provolone left out in the rain.

Barry followed after her, happy to be on dry land. Everyone waited eagerly to see Anna Winmouse — but out came Nicky instead!

"Where is Anna?" wondered one of the reporters.

Ruby and Barry just shrugged. The disappointed reporters began to pack up all their cameras and head back to the parking lot.

The Thea Sisters rushed up to Nicky, who had a small smile on her face. She looked like a mouselet who had scored the **LAST** piece of cheese! She gathered her friends closely around her. "Anna is waiting for us in a nearby cove," she

Sigh!

whispered. "Professor Sparkle took her in the lifeguard boat so the **reporters** wouldn't see her."

"Sneaky!" Pam said.

The THEA SISTERS changed out of their wet clothes and then piled into Pam's jeep to go meet Anna Winmouse at the cove. They found Anna standing under the shade of a pavilion.

Surrounded by her new friends, the Thea Sisters, Anna Winmouse made a big announcement. "I have decided I will grant an EXCLUSIVE interview to one newspaper so that EVERYONE will stop harassing me."

"But how will you choose which one?" Nicky asked.

"Easy-cheesy! I want to be in the academy newspaper, of course!" Anna Winmouse cried. "It will make your SUMMER ISSUE sell like cheese puffs!"

But Anna Winmouse wasn't finished. "I would also love to do a story on you mouselets in **COSMOUSE**!"

The Thea Sisters gasped, delighted. They all hugged Anna in thanks.

"My trip to Whale Island really has been inspirational," Anna said. "And no one has inspired me more than the Thea Sisters!"

Don't miss any of these exciting Thea Sisters adventures!

Thea Stilton and the
Dragon's Code

Thea Stilton and the
Mountain of Fire

Thea Stilton and the
Ghost of the Shipwreck

Thea Stilton and the
Secret City

Thea Stilton and the
Mystery in Paris

Thea Stilton and the
Cherry Blossom Adventure

Thea Stilton and the
Star Castaways

Thea Stilton: Big Trouble
in the Big Apple

Thea Stilton and the
Ice Treasure

Thea Stilton and the
Secret of the Old Castle

Thea Stilton and the
Blue Scarab Hunt

Thea Stilton and the
Prince's Emerald

Thea Stilton and the Mystery
on the Orient Express

Thea Stilton and the
Dancing Shadows

Thea Stilton and the
Legend of the Fire Flowers

Thea Stilton and the
Spanish Dance Mission

Thea Stilton and the
Journey to the Lion's Den

Thea Stilton and the
Great Tulip Heist

Thea Stilton and the
Chocolate Sabotage

Thea Stilton and the
Missing Myth

Thea Stilton and the
Lost Letters

Thea Stilton and the
Tropical Treasure

THE KINGDOM OF FANTASY

THE QUEST FOR PARADISE:
THE RETURN TO THE KINGDOM OF FANTASY

THE AMAZING VOYAGE:
THE THIRD ADVENTURE IN THE KINGDOM OF FANTASY

THE DRAGON PROPHECY:
THE FOURTH ADVENTURE IN THE KINGDOM OF FANTASY

THE VOLCANO OF FIRE:
THE FIFTH ADVENTURE IN THE KINGDOM OF FANTASY

THE SEARCH FOR TREASURE:
THE SIXTH ADVENTURE IN THE KINGDOM OF FANTASY

THE ENCHANTED CHARMS
THE SEVENTH ADVENTURE IN THE KINGDOM OF FANTASY

THE PHOENIX OF DESTINY:
AN EPIC KINGDOM OF FANTASY ADVENTURE

THEA STILTON: THE JOURNEY TO ATLANTIS

THEA STILTON: THE SECRET OF THE FAIRIES

THEA STILTON: THE SECRET OF THE SNOW

THEA STILTON: THE CLOUD CASTLE

Be sure to read all my fabumouse adventures!

#1 Lost Treasure of the Emerald Eye

#2 The Curse of the Cheese Pyramid

#3 Cat and Mouse in a Haunted House

#4 I'm Too Fond of My Fur!

#5 Four Mice Deep in the Jungle

#6 Paws Off, Cheddarface!

#7 Red Pizzas for a Blue Count

#8 Attack of the Bandit Cats

#9 A Fabumouse Vacation for Geronimo

#10 All Because of a Cup of Coffee

#11 It's Halloween, You 'Fraidy Mouse!

#12 Merry Christmas, Geronimo!

#13 The Phantom of the Subway

#14 The Temple of the Ruby of Fire

#15 The Mona Mousa Code

#16 A Cheese-Colored Camper

#17 Watch Your Whiskers, Stilton!

#18 Shipwreck on the Pirate Islands

#19 My Name Is Stilton, Geronimo Stilton

#20 Surf's Up, Geronimo!

#21 The Wild, Wild West

#22 The Secret of Cacklefur Castle

A Christmas Tale

#23 Valentine's Day Disaster

#24 Field Trip to Niagara Falls

#25 The Search for Sunken Treasure

#26 The Mummy with No Name

#27 The Christmas Toy Factory

#28 Wedding Crasher

#29 Down and Out Down Under

#30 The Mouse Island Marathon

#31 The Mysterious Cheese Thief

Christmas Catastrophe

#32 Valley of the Giant Skeletons

#33 Geronimo and the Gold Medal Mystery

#34 Geronimo Stilton, Secret Agent

#35 A Very Merry Christmas

#36 Geronimo's Valentine

#37 The Race Across America

#38 A Fabumouse School Adventure

#39 Singing Sensation

#40 The Karate Mouse

#41 Mighty Mount Kilimanjaro

#42 The Peculiar Pumpkin Thief

#43 I'm Not a Supermouse!

#44 The Giant
Diamond Robbery

#45 Save the White
Whale!

#46 The Haunted
Castle

#47 Run for the Hills,
Geronimo!

#48 The Mystery in
Venice

#49 The Way of
the Samurai

#50 This Hotel Is
Haunted!

#51 The Enormouse
Pearl Heist

#52 Mouse in Space!

#53 Rumble in
the Jungle

#54 Get into Gear,
Stilton!

#55 The Golden
Statue Plot

#56 Flight of the
Red Bandit

The Hunt for the
Golden Book

#57 The Stinky
Cheese Vacation

#58 The Super
Chef Contest

#59 Welcome to
Moldy Manor

The Hunt for the
Curious Cheese

#60 The Treasure of
Easter Island

#61 Mouse House
Hunter

#62 Mouse
Overboard!

Don't miss
my journeys
through time!

Meet
CREEPELLA VON CACKLEFUR

I, *Geronimo Stilton*, have a lot of mouse friends, but none as **spooky** as my friend CREEPELLA VON CACKLEFUR! She is an enchanting and MYSTERIOUS mouse with a pet bat named Bitewing. YIKES! I'm a real 'fraidy mouse, but even I think CREEPELLA and her family are AWFULLY fascinating. I can't wait for you to read all about CREEPELLA in these fa-mouse-ly funny and **spectacularly spooky** tales!

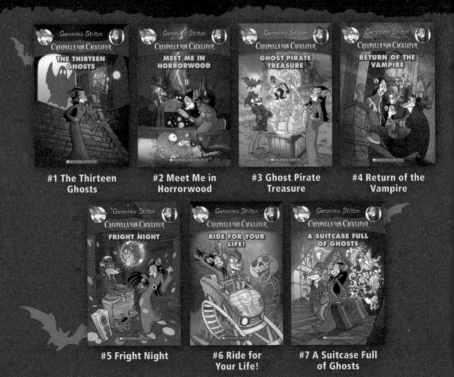

#1 The Thirteen Ghosts

#2 Meet Me in Horrorwood

#3 Ghost Pirate Treasure

#4 Return of the Vampire

#5 Fright Night

#6 Ride for Your Life!

#7 A Suitcase Full of Ghosts

MEET
GERONIMO STILTONIX

He is a spacemouse — the Geronimo
Stilton of a parallel universe! He is
captain of the spaceship *MouseStar 1*.
While flying through the cosmos, he visits
distant planets and meets crazy aliens.
His adventures are out of this world!

#1 Alien Escape

#2 You're Mine, Captain!

#3 Ice Planet Adventure

#4 The Galactic Goal

#5 Rescue Rebellion

#6 The Underwater
Planet

HERB GARDEN

NORTH TOWER

HEADMASTER'S OFFICE

CAFETERIA

GREAT HALL

MOUSEFORD

CLASSROOMS

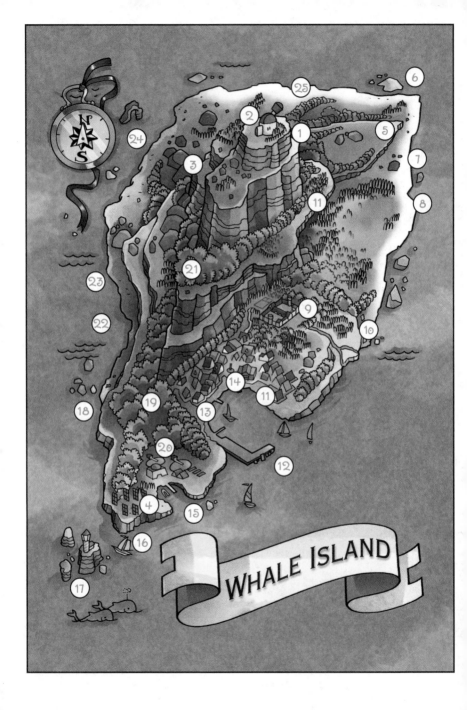

MAP OF
WHALE ISLAND

1. Falcon Peak
2. Observatory
3. Mount Landslide
4. Solar Energy Plant
5. Ram Plain
6. Very Windy Point
7. Turtle Beach
8. Beachy Beach
9. Mouseford Academy
10. Kneecap River
11. Mariner's Inn
12. Port
13. Squid House
14. Town Square
15. Butterfly Bay
16. Mussel Point
17. Lighthouse Cliff
18. Pelican Cliff
19. Nightingale Woods
20. Marine Biology Lab
21. Hawk Woods
22. Windy Grotto
23. Seal Grotto
24. Seagulls Bay
25. Seashell Beach

THANKS FOR READING, AND GOOD-BYE UNTIL OUR NEXT ADVENTURE!

Thea Sisters